THE SERIES

Welcome to Galar!

Adapted by R. Shapiro

ISBN 978-1-338-59307-5

10 9 8 7 6 5 4 3   21 22 23 24
Printed in the U.S.A.   40
First printing 2020
Book design by Cheung Tai

SCHOLASTIC INC.

"There it is! The Galar region!" Goh said.
He pointed out the airplane window.

"Whoa . . ." Ash said. He and Pikachu looked out the window.

The friends were traveling to Galar for the first time. They were excited to explore the new region!

Next, Ash and Goh needed to catch a train
to visit the Wild Area.
But they had to wait three hours before
the train left!

"Why don't we go find some food?" Ash asked.

"I'm in!" Goh replied.

Ash and Pikachu
sniffed the air.
They found a store
selling food.

"What are those tiny things with the awesome smell?" Ash asked.

"Scones," Goh said.

They bought some.

"So yummy!" Ash said.

Suddenly, a rock flew through the air.
"Huh?" Ash and Goh said in surprise.
A playful Pokémon ran by them!

Ash tried to take a picture.
He and Goh didn't notice three Nickit nearby.
The Nickit wanted the extra scones.
They stole Ash's backpack and ran away!

The playful Pokémon ran away, too.
Ash and Goh realized it was friends
with the Nickit.

"Our train tickets are in your backpack, too, aren't they?" Goh asked.

"Yes!" Ash cried.

They chased the Pokémon.

"Which way did they go?" Ash asked.

They heard a bell ring and followed the sound.

Oh no! The Pokémon had led them to a dead end.

Ash and Goh split up to find the backpack.
But Ash got lost! "Piiikachu!" Pikachu said,
worried.

Luckily, Goh found the Pokémon. He called for Ash.

Goh's Rotom told them the name of Nickit, the Fox Pokémon.

But it did not recognize the other Pokémon.

"A new Pokémon species!" Ash and Goh cried. They were excited.

They watched the unknown Pokémon
share scones with the three Nickit.
"It seems like a good friend," Goh said.

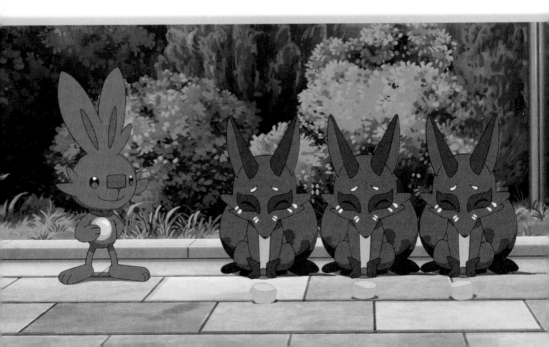

But Ash was angry.

"Those scones belong to me!" he yelled.

"That backpack is mine!"

The mystery Pokémon kicked Ash's backpack.

It got stuck high in the air.

"Give me back my backpack!" Ash shouted.

It looked like the Pokémon was going to attack Ash!

Luckily, his pal Pikachu blocked it.

The battle was on!

"Use Iron Tail!" Ash told Pikachu.

The other Pokémon attacked, but Pikachu dodged its move.

"Pikachu, Thunderbolt! Let's go!" Ash said.

The other Pokémon dodged and did Quick Attack.

"Use Electroweb!" Ash cried.

Pikachu's Electroweb landed.

"We did it, Pikachu!" Ash cheered.

Pikachu climbed up and got Ash's backpack down.

The other Pokémon was not happy.
It gave Ash a huge kick!
"You've got some great moves!" Goh said.

Just then, the three Nickit ran by with more stolen food.

A shopkeeper followed. He grabbed the unknown Pokémon.

Goh didn't want the Pokémon to get in trouble.

"That's my Pokémon!" he said.

"I'll make sure it never does anything like that again!"

The shopkeeper knew Goh was not telling the truth.

"Why would you fib about Scorbunny like that?" he asked.

"Scorbunny?" Goh asked.

Rotom told him the facts about the Rabbit Pokémon.

"Its fur is a different color," Goh said.

"Scorbunny covers itself in mud," the shopkeeper said. "That's why it looks brown. The Nickit are always hungry. Scorbunny is their friend. It helps them get by."

But the shopkeeper did not like that the
Pokémon stole food from people in town.
Scorbunny looked ashamed.
Goh was worried. Scorbunny was really sad.

Goh wanted the Scorbunny to have a better life.
"Please don't give up," he told the little Pokémon.
"It's a big world out there. You can go anywhere
you want to go!"

It was time for Ash and Goh to catch their train.

They waved good-bye to their new friends and ran off.

The Nickit brought Scorbunny to the train, too.

Scorbunny wanted to explore the world, just like Goh said.

The little Pokémon climbed onboard.

It was ready for its next adventure!